D1100796

Fat Alphie the Famous

Fat Alphie and Charlie the Wimp

Make friends with the greatest alley cats in town!

Be sure to read:

The Disappearing Dinner
Fat Alphie in Love
New Kit on the Block
... and lots, lots more!

Fat Alphie the Famous

Margaret Ryan
illustrated by Jacqueline East

■SCHOLASTIC

For Suzy, with love – M.R.

Scholastic Children's Books,
Commonwealth House, 1-19 New Oxford Street,
London, WC1A 1NU, UK
a division of Scholastic Ltd
London ~ New York ~ Toronto ~ Sydney ~ Auckland
Mexico City ~ New Delhi ~ Hong Kong

First published by Scholastic Ltd, 2003

Text copyright © Margaret Ryan, 2003
Illustrations copyright © Jacqueline East, 2003

ISBN 0 439 97810 6

Printed and bound by Oriental Press, Dubai, UAE

10 9 8 7 6 5 4 3 2 1

The rights of Margaret Ryan and Jacqueline East to be identified as the author and
illustrator of this work respectively have been asserted by them in accordance with the
Copyright, Designs and Patents Act, 1988.

Chapter One

It was a fine morning in Little Yowling. Fat Alphie yawned and stretched and was just going back to sleep when Charlie the Wimp brought in the mail. "Letter for you," he said.

Fat Alphie opened it up.

"It's from my cousin, Skinny Jinny. She's in the middle of a swamp in darkest Africa," he said. "Can't think what she's doing there, in all that mud."

"Not Skinny Jinny, the famous explorer!" said Charlie the Wimp. "She's fantastic. Imagine having a famous explorer in the family. What's she like?"

"Thin," said Fat Alphie. "And bossy.
Anyway, being famous isn't so special.
I could be famous if I wanted."

"Famous for what?" said Charlie the
Wimp. "Eating doesn't count."

"Just wait," said Fat Alphie. "I'll think
of something. You'll see."

Fat Alphie
got up and ate
two tins of
sardines.

Then he strolled down Main Street.
Charlie the Wimp stayed close behind.

Suddenly Fat Alphie stopped. "Look at that, Charlie," he said.

An artist was drawing a magnificent Spanish galleon on the pavement.

"I could do that," said Fat Alphie. "I could be a famous pavement artist. But first I need some chalk. Come on, Charlie. I know where we can get some."

"I had a feeling you might," sighed Charlie.

Fat Alphie led Charlie the Wimp to the bin behind Little Yowling Primary School.

"In you go, Charlie," he said. "There's bound to be some chalk in there."

"Why do I have to go?" moaned Charlie as he climbed up.

"Because you're smaller than me," said Fat Alphie. He gave Charlie a push and he fell head first into the bin. SQUELCH.

He came up covered in school dinner custard. But he WAS holding two pieces of chalk.

"Is that all you could get?" tutted Fat Alphie. "Well, I suppose it will have to do."

Fat Alphie chose a piece of pavement and began to draw.

"Is that supposed to be a ship?" muttered Charlie.

"It's got too many masts," said Millie the Mouser, strolling past.

"And not enough sails," said One-eared Tom.

"Is it a ship or a shop?" said Clever Claws.

13

"Well, I think it's lovely," sniffed Fat Alphie. He was just adding a little flag when it started to rain and his picture was washed away.

"Oh no," cried Fat Alphie. "My beautiful drawing! It's a hard life being a famous artist."

Charlie rolled his eyes and said nothing.

The two cats sheltered in a doorway till the rain stopped.

Then Fat Alphie strolled on down Main Street. Charlie the Wimp stayed close behind.

Suddenly Fat Alphie stopped.
"Look at that, Charlie," he said.

An artist was painting a
football match on
the side of a house.

"I could do that," said Fat Alphie. "I could be a famous street artist. But first I need a brush and some paint. Come on, Charlie. I know where we can get some."

"I had a feeling you might," muttered Charlie.

Fat Alphie led Charlie the Wimp to the bin behind the decorator's shop.

Dotty's Design

"In you go, Charlie," he said. "There's bound to be a brush and some tins of paint in there."

"Why do I have to go?" moaned Charlie, as he climbed up.

"Because you're fitter than me," said Fat Alphie. He gave Charlie a poke and he fell head first into the bin.

SPLOOSH.

He came up covered in whitewash. But he WAS holding a brush and a tin of paint.

"Is that all you could get?" tutted Fat Alphie. "Well, I suppose it will have to do."

Fat Alphie chose the side of a coal shed and began to paint.

"Is that supposed to be a football match?" muttered Charlie the Wimp.

"The players have got too many legs," said Millie the Mouser, strolling past.

"And not enough arms," said One-eared Tom.

"The centre forward is offside," said Clever Claws.

"Well, I think
it's lovely,"
sniffed Fat Alphie.
He was just
adding the referee
when it started to
rain and his picture
was washed away.

"Oh no," cried Fat Alphie. "My beautiful
painting! It's a hard life being
a famous artist."

Charlie the Wimp
rolled his eyes,
sighed and
said nothing.

The two cats
sheltered under
a hedge till the
rain stopped.

Then Fat Alphie
strolled on down
Main Street. Charlie the Wimp stayed close
behind. Suddenly Fat Alphie stopped.

"Look at that, Charlie," he said.

By the side of the road an artist was
drawing an old
oak tree.

"I could do that," said Fat Alphie. "I could be a famous sketch artist. But first I need some paper and a pencil. Come on, Charlie. I know where we can get some."

"I had a feeling you might," muttered Charlie.

Fat Alphie led Charlie to the bin behind the stationer's.

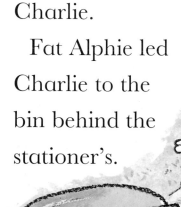

"In you go, Charlie," he said. "There's bound to be some paper and pencils in there."

"Why do I have to go?" moaned Charlie as he climbed up.

"Because you're lighter than me," said Fat Alphie. He gave Charlie a prod and he fell head first into the bin.

ICKY STICKY.

Papermates

He came up covered
in glue and bits of
string. But he WAS
holding a pencil and
a piece of paper.

"Is that all you
could get?" tutted
Fat Alphie. "Well,
I suppose it will have to do."

Fat Alphie chose another large oak and
began to sketch.

"Is that supposed to be a tree?"
said Charlie the Wimp.

"It's far too tall," said Millie the Mouser, strolling past.

"And far too thin," said One-eared Tom.

"A puff of wind would blow that tree down," said Clever Claws.

Just then a puff of wind came along and blew the drawing up into the air and over the roof tops.

"Oh no," cried Fat Alphie. "My beautiful sketch! Now what am I going to do? It's a very hard life being a famous artist!"

Charlie the Wimp rolled his eyes, sighed, shook his head and said nothing.

 🐾 Chapter Two 🐾

Back home at number three Wheelie Bin
Avenue, Fat Alphie was still feeling glum.

He nibbled some fish and chips from a
newspaper and sighed.

"How am I ever going to be a famous
artist if all my work disappears, Charlie?" he
said. "It's enough to put me off my food!"

Charlie the Wimp looked at the
newspaper Fat Alphie was licking clean.
"No it's not," he muttered.

"Wait a minute, Charlie," said Fat Alphie
as he took one last lick. "Look at this."

There was a
big notice on
the front page
of the newspaper.

**CALLING ALL ARTISTS!
PAINTING COMPETITION**

Paint a portrait to hang
in Little Yowling's Town Hall
Win a HUGE hamper of food!

"I could enter
that competition,"
said Fat Alphie.
"I'm an artist.
But first I need
some tubes of
paint and a canvas,

and I know where we can get some."

"I had a feeling you might," said Charlie.

Next morning Fat Alphie led Charlie to
the bin behind the art shop.

POTS AND
PAINTS

"In you go, Charlie," he said. "There's bound to be a canvas and some tubes of paint in there."

"Why do I always have to go," moaned Charlie as he climbed up.

"Because you're thinner than me," said Fat Alphie. He gave Charlie a nudge and he fell head first into the bin. SPLAT.

He came up covered in every colour of paint under the sun. But he WAS holding a canvas

and several half-squeezed tubes of paint.

"Splendid, splendid," cried Fat Alphie. "Now be careful not to drop them on the way home."

Back at number three Wheelie Bin Avenue, Fat Alphie sat Charlie on top of the armchair. He arranged his paws and his tail, and began to paint his portrait.

"Sit very still, Charlie," he said, "so that
I can get a good likeness."
Charlie the Wimp
sat very still.

Then he wriggled.

He sat very still.
Then he sneezed.

He sat very still.
Then he coughed.
He sat very still.
Then he coughed
and sneezed
and wriggled.

Fat Alphie sighed and put down his brush.

"Can't you sit still for more than one minute at a time?" he complained. "What's the matter with you? Have you got ants in your pants?"

"No," said Charlie, looking down. "But
I have got them crawling up my leg. Help!
Help!" And he danced about on top of the
armchair to get rid of them.

"How am I supposed to paint your
portrait if you can't sit still," muttered Fat
Alphie. "It's a very, very hard life being an
artist."

Chapter Three

When the portrait was finished, Fat Alphie
wrapped it up in some old newspaper,
tied it with string, and handed it in to the
town hall.

Then he nibbled
his claws and
waited.

The judging of the paintings was two
days later. Millie the Mouser, One-eared
Tom and Clever Claws followed Fat Alphie
and Charlie the Wimp down to the town
hall to have a look.

"There are a lot of portraits," worried Fat Alphie.

"Some of them are very smiley," said Millie the Mouser.

"Some of them are very glum," said One-eared Tom.

"But all of them have two eyes, two ears, a mouth and a nose," said Clever Claws. "Except this one."

"It's only got one eye," said Millie the Mouser.

"And two noses," said One-eared Tom.

"It's got a mouth where an ear should be," said Clever Claws.

My Best Friend, Charlie the Wimp

"And it's called 'My Best Friend, Charlie the Wimp'," squeaked Charlie. "Is that supposed to be me!"

"I did my best," sniffed Fat Alphie. "You wouldn't sit still."

Just then the Lord Mayor appeared in his fancy robes and hat to judge the portraits. He walked slowly down the long line of paintings.

"Very interesting. Very interesting indeed," he said, as he looked at them closely. "But they're all very much the same. Except this one."

He stood in front of the portrait of Charlie the Wimp and smiled. "This reminds me of that famous artist, Picasso. This portrait, 'My Best Friend, Charlie the Wimp', is definitely the winner."

Fat Alphie jumped up and down. "I've won. I've won," he cried, as the Lord Mayor shook him by the paw.

Fat Alphie talked about nothing else all the way home.

"Did you hear what the Lord Mayor said, Charlie?" he asked for the umpteenth time. "I'm a famous artist. I shall write and tell Skinny Jinny right away. She's not the only famous one in the family now. What do you think about that?"

"I think a famous artist could help carry his prize home," said Charlie, staggering under the weight of the hamper.

"And risk damaging my famous paws? Don't be silly, Charlie," said Fat Alphie. "It's a very nice life being a famous artist!"